THE EASTER EGG FARM

written and illustrated by

MARY JANE AUCH

Holiday House / New York

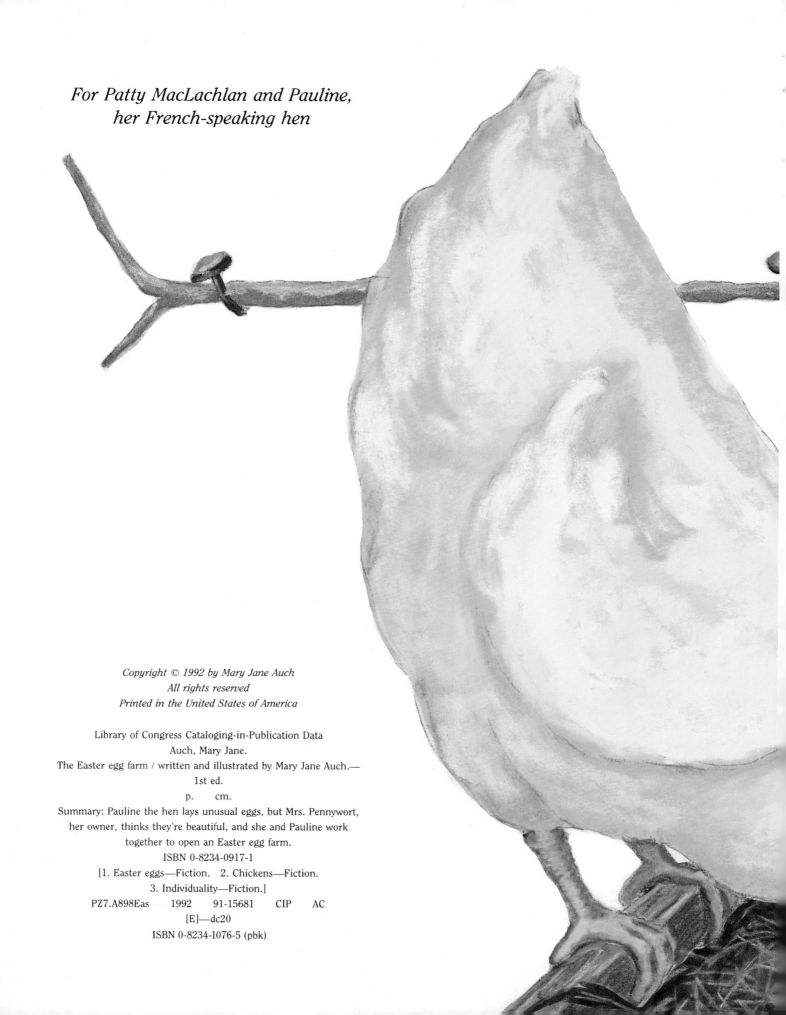

For Patty MacLachlan and Pauline,
her French-speaking hen

Library of Congress Cataloging-in-Publication Data
Auch, Mary Jane.
The Easter egg farm / written and illustrated by Mary Jane Auch.—
1st ed.
p.   cm.
Summary: Pauline the hen lays unusual eggs, but Mrs. Pennywort,
her owner, thinks they're beautiful, and she and Pauline work
together to open an Easter egg farm.
ISBN 0-8234-0917-1
[1. Easter eggs—Fiction. 2. Chickens—Fiction.
3. Individuality—Fiction.]
PZ7.A898Eas   1992   91-15681   CIP   AC
[E]—dc20
ISBN 0-8234-1076-5 (pbk)

Pauline lived in Mrs. Pennywort's henhouse with four other hens.

Each day, Mrs. Pennywort collected the eggs. "Only four eggs again today?" she asked. "Somebody isn't doing her job. Are you all trying?"

The hens clucked.

"Well, try harder. I want five eggs tomorrow. Concentrate!"

Pauline was embarrassed. She was the one not laying an egg. Every time she tried, the other hens squabbled. Pauline couldn't concentrate in all the confusion.

"Pauline is lazy," one hen clucked.
"I'm not lazy," Pauline said.
"I'm just different." She
turned her back on the
others and concentrated
very hard.

Finally, a wonderful thing happened. Pauline stepped back to look at the egg in her nest. It wasn't like the other eggs, but Pauline thought it was beautiful.

"Get a load of this," another hen cackled. "Pauline just laid the world's ugliest egg."

"It's not ugly," Pauline said. "It's just different." But Pauline began to feel ashamed of her egg. She nudged it under the straw with her beak.

The harder Pauline tried to lay a normal egg, the stranger her eggs got. She hid each one of them, but not before the other hens had seen them and made fun of her.

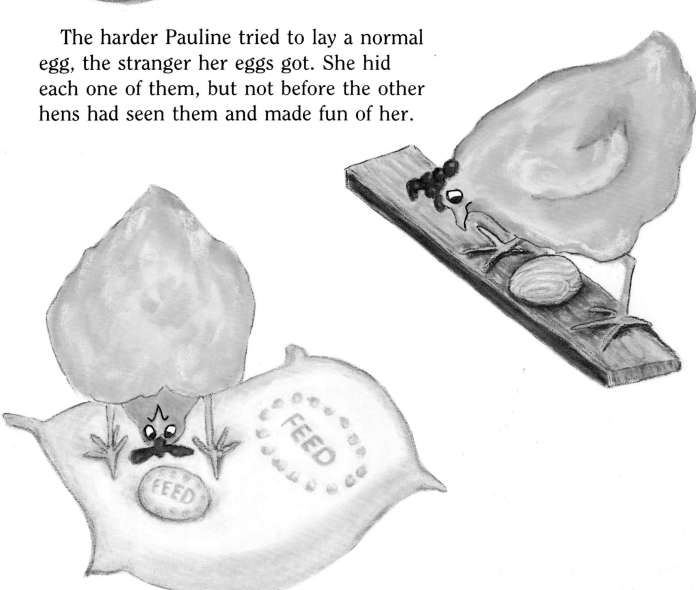

When Pauline couldn't stand the teasing any longer, she made herself a nest outdoors. She stared at the sky, concentrating very hard. This time her egg came out blue with clouds. But before Pauline could hide the egg, someone saw it—Mrs. Pennywort.

"Pauline, what a lovely egg," she said, holding it up in the sunshine. "This is too unusual to crack open for my breakfast. I'll put it on my windowsill where everybody can enjoy it."

The next day, Pauline laid an egg that was even more unusual. Mrs. Pennywort was delighted. "Can you make more eggs like this?" Then Mrs. Pennywort noticed the ladybug on a blade of grass right in front of Pauline. "Hey, I get it. The egg comes out looking like whatever you see, right?"

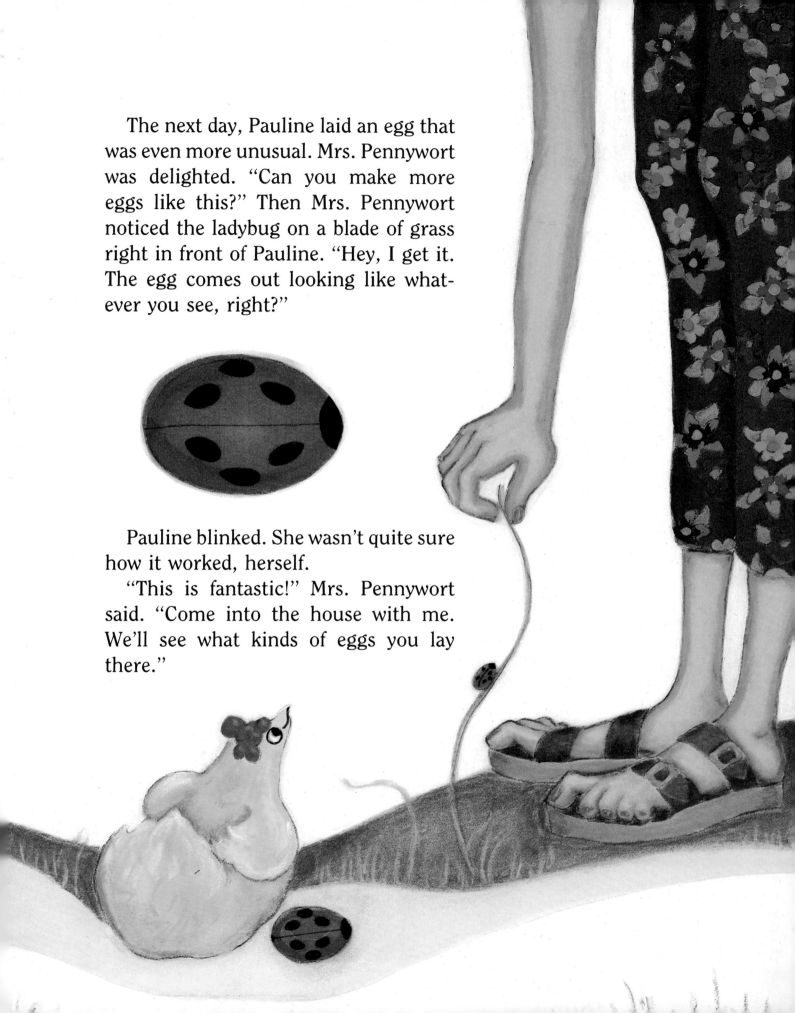

Pauline blinked. She wasn't quite sure how it worked, herself.

"This is fantastic!" Mrs. Pennywort said. "Come into the house with me. We'll see what kinds of eggs you lay there."

Pauline loved being inside. There were lots of pretty things to look at. In her new surroundings, Pauline became quite creative. Soon her unusual eggs lined the windowsills of Mrs. Pennywort's house.

One day, a lady appeared at the window. "Are these lovely Easter eggs for sale? I need one for every child in town. They're for the annual Easter egg hunt."

"No problem. We can lay that many eggs, can't we, Pauline?"

We? thought Pauline. She'd never seen Mrs. Pennywort lay an egg, so she knew it was up to her. Laying eggs for the Easter egg hunt would be an honor. She clucked happily.

"Come back for your eggs the night before Easter," said Mrs. Pennywort.

Pauline was excited. She started laying two eggs a day, then three, then four. Mrs. Pennywort began taking Pauline on field trips for inspiration.

The first week, they went to the art museum.

The second week, they went to the ballet. Pauline was so thrilled by the music and dancing, she laid more eggs than ever when they got home.

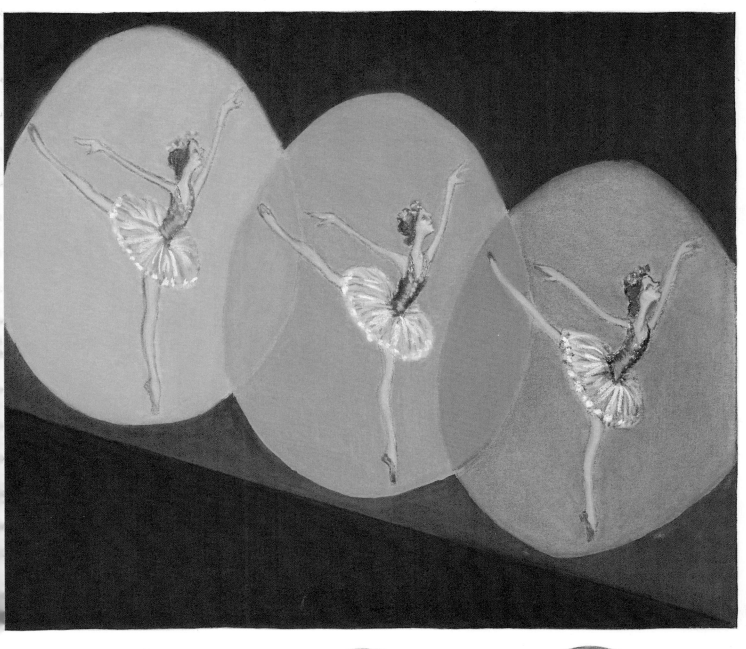

Finally, it was the day before Easter. "The egg lady will be here tonight," said Mrs. Pennywort. "I'd better start packing up the eggs." She lifted an egg from the windowsill. "Uh-oh! There's a crack in this shell."

Mrs. Pennywort ran to another window. "Pauline, some of the eggs are hatching! We shouldn't have left them in the sunshine!"

Soon baby chicks were popping out all over the sunny side of the house.

"Stay in there!" Mrs. Pennywort shouted at the unhatched chicks. "You're ruining the eggs." But the chicks didn't listen. They just kept hatching and hatching.

Mrs. Pennywort took the broken shells to the table and frantically tried to glue them together. "It's no use. I was never any good at craft projects."

Just then, there was a knock at the door. "Yoo-hoo!" called the egg lady. "I'm here for the Easter eggs."

"Do I have a deal for you!" cried Mrs. Pennywort. "How would you like Easter chicks instead of eggs?"

"Terrific!" the egg lady said, as bright-colored chicks scurried around her. "Easter chicks are even better than Easter eggs."

Mrs. Pennywort helped the egg lady gather the chicks. But as fast as they were popped into a basket, the chicks jumped out again. Mrs. Pennywort heard a clucking noise and looked up.

Pauline was fluffed up to twice her normal size. She spread her wings like an umbrella, protecting the chicks who raced toward her.

"Oh, Pauline," said Mrs. Pennywort, "of course we can't give away the chicks. They're your babies!"

"But what about the Easter Egg hunt?" the egg lady asked.

"The eggs on the shady side of the house didn't hatch," Mrs. Pennywort said. "You can take those."

Pauline kept all of her babies. She loved being a mother. Every day she took her chicks for a walk, showing them the beautiful things around the farm.

The chicks' grown-up feathers started to come in. "These chicks sure are different," said Mrs. Pennywort.

Pauline clucked proudly.

Soon Pauline's daughters were laying their own eggs. They took turns in the nest box, laying eggs of every color and design. Children from miles around came to see the unusual eggs and chickens. Mrs. Pennywort's farm became known as The Easter Egg Farm.

Pauline still lives on The Easter Egg Farm, but she doesn't lay as many eggs as she used to. Now, whenever she feels an egg coming on, Pauline closes her eyes. She doesn't concentrate on anything. Then she lays a perfectly ordinary, plain white egg—just to be different.